EGYPTIAN TREASURE TOMB

by Jack D. Clifford

Illustrated by Russ Daff

W
FRANKLIN WATTS
LONDON•SYDNEY

Jack and Emily had a new game.

They were looking for treasure

in an Egyptian tomb.

"Got the map!" shouted Jack.

"Got the rope!" shouted Emily.

Suddenly, a red light shone ...

"What happened?" cried Jack.

"I think we're inside the game,"
Emily replied.

Footsteps thumped towards them.

They got louder and louder.

"Get down!" whispered Emily.

"Without the stone of peace, Queen Kiya cannot stop the war!" growled a gruff voice.

"She'll never find it!" sneered a different voice. "In half an hour, this tomb will be closed forever."

The footsteps thumped away.

"Here's the stone of peace,"

said Jack. "Look, it's on the map."

"We must find it," replied Emily.

"And get out before the tomb

is closed!"

"We're here. The map shows the stone in a chamber below us," Jack said.

"Let's try this corridor,"

said Emily.

Jack and Emily rushed down the
corridor to the next chamber.

"The map shows a way down,
but I can't see it," said Jack.

"Look," said Emily.

"Here's a patch of sand."

As she brushed away the

sand, an opening appeared.

"How do you get down there?"

asked Jack.

"With the rope!" replied Emily.

Emily held onto the rope, while Jack
climbed down into the tiny chamber.

"Found the stone!" cried Jack.

"Let's get out of here!"

"This way! Quick!" said Emily.

Jack and Emily raced through
corridor after corridor.

Then the floor fell away beneath them,

and they tumbled ...

... out of the tomb, into the cold desert

evening. Jack and Emily looked around.

"That must be Queen Kiya!" shouted

Emily. "Throw the stone to her!"

25

"The stone of peace!" cried Queen
Kiya. "You've saved us all! How can
we thank you?"

Before Jack or Emily could reply,

a red light shone ...

... and they were back home.

"That was a great game!"

they laughed.

PUZZLE TIME

Can you put these pictures

in the correct order?

TURN OVER FOR ANSWERS!

Tell the story in your own words
with YOU as the hero!

ANSWERS

The correct order is: d, b, a, c.

First published in 2011 by
Franklin Watts
338 Euston Road
London
NW1 3BH

Franklin Watts Australia
Level 17/207 Kent Street
Sydney
NSW 2000

Text © Jack D. Clifford 2011
Illustration © Russ Daff 2011

A CIP catalogue record for this book is
available from the British Library.

ISBN 978 1 4451 0304 4 (hbk)
ISBN 978 1 4451 0312 9 (pbk)

Series Editor: Jackie Hamley
Series Advisor: Catherine Glavina
Series Designer: Peter Scoulding

Printed in China

Franklin Watts is a division of Hachette
Children's Books, an Hachette UK company.
www.hachette.co.uk